For Paul, with gratitude for our wild-peace life —I. L.
For Mr. and Mrs. Hull's new adventure —I. S. N.

Published by Roaring Brook Press
Roaring Brook Press is a division of Holtzbrinck Publishing Holdings Limited Partnership
120 Broadway, New York, NY 10271 • mackids.com

Text copyright © 2021 by Irene Latham
Illustrations copyright © 2021 by Il Sung Na

Library of Congress Cataloging-in-Publication Data is available.
ISBN 978-1-250-31042-2

Our books may be purchased in bulk for promotional, educational, or business use.
Please contact your local bookseller or the Macmillan Corporate and Premium Sales Department
at (800) 221-7945 ext. 5442 or by email at MacmillanSpecialMarkets@macmillan.com.

First edition, 2021 • Book design by Mercedes Padró
The art for this book was created with Adobe Fresco.
Printed in China by RR Donnelley Asia Printing Solutions Ltd.,
Dongguan City, Guangdong Province

1 3 5 7 9 10 8 6 4 2

WILD PEACE

written by
Irene Latham

illustrated by
Il Sung Na

Roaring Brook Press
New York

When the world fills with noise and fury,

and the days pass,
all rush and scurry,

it's time to step into the forest.

Into the forest,

where peace trills *good morning* to the sky
and watches the web dry.

Peace gathers as many
nuts as it can carry

and feasts on a perfect berry.

Peace rises on
spindly legs

and coils around
a nest of eggs.

Peace hop-stops,

hop-stops,

hop-stops,

hops.

Peace buzzes a
sticky-sweet tune

and gnaws on logs
all afternoon.

Peace presses forever upstream
and perches in the sun to dream.

Peace towers.

Peace showers.

Peace grows in a clump

and hides behind a stump.

Peace swoops across twilight
and brightens the bluest night.

Peace welcomes all that is wild

and kisses the forehead
of each and every child.